HOW TO RAISE CHILDREN'S SELF-ESTEEM

by
Harris Clemes, Ph.D.
Reynold Bean, Ed.M.

Edited by
Janet Gluckman

ENRICH™
Education Division of
PRICE STERN SLOAN, INC.

1980 revised edition

ISBN: 0-8431-2525-X

20 19 18 17 16 15 14 13 12 11 10

CONTENTS

INTRODUCTION

Self-esteem is the basis for positive growth in human relations, learning, creativity, and personal responsibility. It is the "cement" that binds children's personalities together into positive, integrated and effective structures. At every stage of a child's life, his* self-esteem determines the degree to which he can use the personal resources and potential he was born with.

Children always do what they do for a reason. Our efforts to guide them in positive ways depend to a considerable extent on our ability to understand the reasons or motives that underlie their actions. Many times these motives are "hidden;" they result from feelings or perceptions that are "inside" a child, and the child may not have the ability to tell us what they are.

Even though parents and teachers can't control everything that happens to children, we can influence broad areas of their activities and respond more appropriately to them when they are experiencing stress in their lives. When children have high self-esteem, they feel good! If their self-esteem is low, they don't. Observing how they behave in different situations is the key that unlocks our understanding of how to help them feel good more often.

Though we all want our children to have high self-esteem, there are times when even our best efforts to provide them with positive feelings of self-worth seem to be useless. When that happens, we become confused and worried.

It is precisely to remove that confusion that this handbook was born. The information contained in it is designed to help you understand your children better and to explain those aspects of their behavior that may seem inconsistent, confusing, or irrational.

— The Authors

---

*He, rather than he or she, is used in the text for the sake of fluidity.

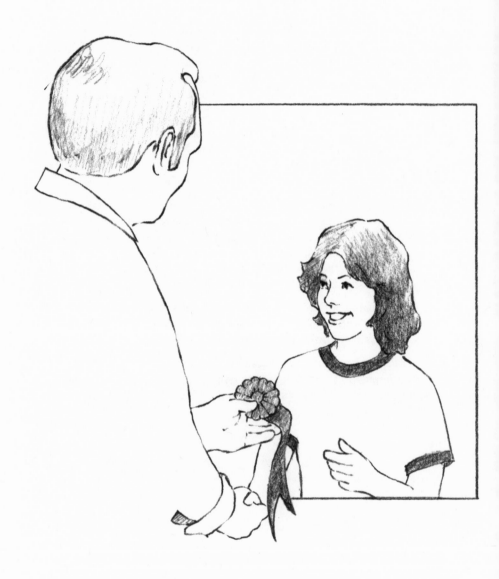

I.
What Is Self-Esteem and Why Is It Important?

This section of the handbook will describe what self-esteem is, and the effect that it has on all parts of a child's life. Children with low self-esteem are no less "handicapped" than people with severe physical disability. When self-esteem is low, the ability to be successful in learning, human relationships, and in all the productive areas of their lives is limited.

What is High Self-Esteem?

Can you remember times when you felt really good about yourself? Chances are that they were characterized by some or all of the following feelings:

- You felt that you were important to someone who was important to you.

- You felt "special," even if you couldn't put your finger on what made you feel that way.

- You felt that you were on top of things, getting done what was needed, and feeling confident that you could handle whatever came your way.

- You felt purposeful—that you were working toward goals that were important to you, which expressed your own beliefs and values.

The feelings you felt are called self-esteem. In those cases they were positive and resulted in actions that tended to reinforce good feelings.

It's important to remember that self-esteem is a feeling that always expresses itself in the way people act. Self-esteem can be observed in children in *what* they do and *how* they do things.

Self-esteem is different from self-concept, though the two ideas are often confused. Self-concept is a "theory," a set of ideas that a child has about himself. Self-concept can often be reported—a child can say what he believes about himself, even though his beliefs may not correspond to his behavior. A child has beliefs about self regarding what he *does* well or poorly, the *preferences* he has about things, what he *likes or dislikes,* the *roles* he plays in relationship to others, and the *standards* he holds. He may believe he's friendly, but have no friends. He may have a preference for sports, but refuse to join teams at school.

Self-concept and self-esteem are related in that a child's sense of personal satisfaction with himself is enhanced when:

- He has successfully expressed his self-concept in performance, i.e. when a child who sees himself as a good athlete hits the game-winning homerun.

- He has lived up to the personal standards associated with his self concept, i.e. when a child who values his academic skills receives the highest score on a math test.

- He has had his self-concept confirmed by others, i.e. when a child who believes he draws well has his painting praised.

The Characteristics of High and Low Self-Esteem

At this point, it will be useful to describe the characteristics of both high and low self-esteem children, in order to illustrate the differences:

A child with high self-esteem will . . .

. . . be proud of his accomplishments:	"Look at this; I really like this picture I painted."
. . . act independently:	"I made my own breakfast."
. . . assume responsibility easily:	"I'll water the plants for you."
. . . tolerate frustration well:	"Boy, this model is hard to put together, but I know I can do it."
. . . approach new challenges with enthusiasm:	"Wow, teacher said that we're going to start learning long division tomorrow."

6

...feel capable of influencing others: "Let me show you how to play this new game I learned."

...exhibit a broad range of emotions and feelings: "I feel so good when Dad's home, and sad when he's gone.

A child with low self-esteem will...

...avoid situations that provoke anxiety: "I'm not going to school today; there's a hard test in math."

...demean his own talents: "Nothing I draw looks any good."

...feel that others don't value him: "They never want to play with me."

...blame others for his own weaknesses: "You didn't tell me where the broom was, so I couldn't clean up the mess."

...be easily influenced by others: "I know I shouldn't have done it, but they dared me to."

...become defensive and easily frustrated: "It's not my fault the kite won't fly— I'm just going to smash the stupid thing."

...feel powerless: "I can't find the scissors; where's the tape? I don't have the right book—I'll *never* finish this project.

...exhibit a narrow range of emotions and feelings: "I don't care; it doesn't make any difference to me what you do."

Self-esteem waxes and wanes. When children have high or low self-esteem they *generally* exhibit the characteristics specified for them above, but all children will show these characteristics at one time or another. The "pattern" of their behavior needs to be observed, rather than focusing on any one characteristic.

Self-Esteem as a Motive for Behavior

Because self-esteem (the way children *feel* about themselves) is related to self-concept (the ideas or beliefs children have about themselves), children are motivated to act in ways that express both. Specifically, there are three major motives affecting behavior that result from beliefs and feelings about self.

1. **A child will act in ways that increase his sense of self-worth and satisfaction.** Some examples of this are: seeking praise and approval,

doing things he likes to do and does well, avoiding tasks that he's likely to fail at, pleasing others.

2. **A child will act in ways that confirm his self-image (concept) by others and himself.** If a child believes he is a "good" boy, he will tend to act well; conversely, if a child thinks he's bad, he will (unconsciously) seek criticism and punishment. If a child believes she's good at sports, she'll want to play at every opportunity. If a child believes he's poor at math, he'll get poor grades in it, and believe any deviation from them is "luck."

3. **A child will act so as to maintain a consistent self-image, irrespective of changing circumstances.** "That's the way I am!" "I've always been like that." It's at least as hard for children as it is for adults to change something about themselves that expresses a basic belief, even though there may be evidence to support a new behavior. Example: a child who can solve math problems in his head may do poorly on tests because he expects to do poorly.

These three *motives* influence the way children behave, and often are expressed simultaneously—even when they conflict! This results in behavior that often seems erratic or irrational. A child might avoid doing something that all indications suggest he could do successfully. An example of this might be the child who reads a lot at home, but does not share this part of himself at school because his image at school is that of a "clown," for which he gets approval from peers. Or children may promise to do something for parents in order to gain approval, but don't follow through because they really don't believe they can do it successfully.

Children can have a "negative" self-concept. This means that, with regard to specific issues or areas of their lives, they believe that they are bad, dumb, sick, unlovable, incompetent. When such negative beliefs are firmly held by a child, he will tend to express them as if they were positive ones—seeking confirmation of them, and maintaining consistency in them.

Children with negative attitudes about themselves tend not to believe evidence to the contrary. They reject praise or approval for things that they hold negative beliefs about. Examples: a child who believes that he is not liked or trusted may reject attempts by teachers or others to convince him that they like him and want to help him; another child who feels that he doesn't measure up to his classmates in some aspect of school work will likely reject evidence of success, dismissing it as luck or a "mistake."

When children have low self-esteem, their behavior reflects it. As patterns develop that are characteristic of low self-esteem, they become habits and are as intractable as any other.

8

Self-Esteem and School Performance

One of the most important factors that influence school success is self-esteem. Children with superior intelligence and low self-esteem can do poorly in school, while children with average intelligence and high self-esteem can be unusually successful. Children with low self-esteem tend to get little satisfaction from school. They lose motivation and interest easily, and tend to focus a good deal of energy on those issues that are affecting their feelings about themselves—relationships with others, problems, fears and anxieties. Less interest is directed toward school tasks.

Often the experiences that reinforce low self-esteem are school related, producing anxieties that the child is continually dealing with. Low self-esteem hinders good school performance, and poor performance leads to low self-esteem.

This becomes like a merry-go-round; it becomes more and more difficult for a child to jump off as time passes.

As children fall farther behind, greater emphasis is placed on remedial activities. They become immersed in a continuing pattern of failure and self denigration, while the special issues of their self-esteem are overlooked.

Anxiety, if excessive, interferes with learning. Low self-esteem children are dealing with issues that result in anxiety and interfere with learning. As self-esteem rises, anxiety diminishes, allowing the child to participate with greater motivation in learning tasks.

Self-Esteem and Interpersonal Relationships

Children with high self-esteem generally have good relationships with others. Such relationships are self perpetuating—both children and adults *like* to relate to someone who is pleasant to relate to. Children with low self-esteem are either overly aggressive or excessively retiring in interpersonal relationships, and thus produce little satisfaction for others.

Relationships are terribly important to a child with low self-esteem. He seeks support and approval from others that he can't give to himself. But such a child will tend to distort communications and misconstrue people's attitudes, believing that others believe about him what he believes about himself. Children's efforts to be friendly toward a child with low self-esteem are often frustrated because of this.

If a child *feels* that he is not liked or valued by others, he will anticipate such attitudes towards himself, *whether the attitudes are there or not.*

9

Self-Esteem and Creativity

Parents and teachers like to see children being creative. Children who keep themselves busy with imaginative play, who say or do things that are unique, and who show some degree of artistic or intellectual talent, are a delight to most adults. The tendency to act creatively is related to a child's self-esteem.

Creativity involves the following factors that are directly influenced by self-esteem:

- Creative acts always involve some degree of risk. A child has to have a high level of self-confidence in order to take risks.

- In order to act creatively a child must trust others—and must know that he'll still be accepted, even if he fails at something.

- Being creative involves the integration of intellect, visual imagery, playfulness, and mental and physical dexterity. If a child is excessively anxious or fearful, because of low self-esteem, such integration is unlikely to occur. Anxiety interferes with the successful expression of all of these capabilities.

- True creativity is something that arises from inside a child and does not occur "on demand." If a child is dependent on praise and approval from other people, he will be more likely to seek to conform to others' wishes.

- Being creative involves a high degree of clarity about one's own mental images or models. Creative children tend to take delight and satisfaction from making such models real (seeing something in their "mind's eye," and making it happen). Anxiety about how others will judge an act, or anticipating failure (both characteristics of children with low self-esteem), undermine a child's ability to experience such personal satisfaction.

Creativity in children is not usually expressed as some awe-inspiring talent, genius or precocious competence. Artistic and intellectually gifted "geniuses" are rare. Creative children express this quality in day-to-day activities, at play and work, in small ways, such as decorating their own rooms, playing spontaneous fantasy games, seeing things from a different perspective (a book becomes a wall of a fort, and sweeping the porch becomes a "war" against dirt).

A child's level of self-esteem determines the amount of creative behavior expressed.

How Parents'/Teachers' Self-Esteem Affects Children

Everyone knows that parents are "models" for their children. But children often copy parents' *feelings and attitudes,* as well as language, mannerisms, and the things that parents *do.* What goes on *inside* of parents is as much a reference point for children as what goes on *outside,* i.e. the ways that parents act. Parents' feelings and attitudes are often expressed in subtle, nonverbal ways. Example: a shrug that is associated with a tense expression may tell a child that a parent is disappointed, even though nothing is said. Incongruities between what is said and the tone of voice used, can communicate an unspoken message. It is almost impossible to hide a feeling, and children become very acute observers of subtle expressions that convey parental attitudes.

Children are always looking to parents for cues about how to behave. When parents have an emotional reaction, even though they may not express it, the child, nevertheless, is influenced by it.

Several interpersonal patterns emerge between parents with low self-esteem and their children. Such patterns produce stresses and result in self-esteem problems in the children.

- Parents with low self-esteem tend to "live" through their children. They want their children to achieve goals that they, themselves, haven't achieved, and are disappointed when their children don't. Their children are caught between trying to live up to the parents' expectations and wanting to do their "own thing."

- Parents with low self-esteem are often anxious. Anxiety distorts communications.

- Parents with low self-esteem are often threatened by high self-esteem in their children, particularly when they seek independence and autonomy. Parents interpret such behavior as rejection of themselves. Children become confused, frustrated, and angry when this happens.

- When parents have low self-esteem they tend to see a problem or a potential problem in everything. Attempting to head off problems that don't yet exist results in having standards and expectations that children have a hard time meeting.

- Low self-esteem parents have difficulty praising realistically and precisely. They tend to praise not at all, very little, or conversely, excessively. The praise they offer is global and general, rather than specific. Children like any kind of praise, but if it is too general, it doesn't give them specific information about their behavior, leading to ambiguity and confusion.

• Parents with low self-esteem tend to give mixed messages to their children about success. They encourage their children toward success, but also imply that it will be ephemeral and temporary. ("Keep trying, but don't expect to win!") If parents are really threatened by their children's success, they may go so far as to undermine the success, by withholding resources, criticizing, or breaking promises.

Parents with low self-esteem *cannot* avoid some of the above dilemmas. They must face themselves squarely before they can effectively enhance their children's self-esteem.

Science
Class B₂
by
Kim Willcox

II.
The Four Conditions of Self-Esteem

Significant experiences and the quality of relationships with people who are important to him greatly influence a child's feelings about himself. Because of this, parents and teachers *can* influence a child's self-esteem in positive ways, by organizing new experiences and relating to the child in appropriate ways.

This section will describe the four conditions that must be met in order for children to have high self-esteem. This material is the basis for succeeding sections that will show you what to do to raise a child's self-esteem.

Self-Esteem and Children's Needs

A child is very much like a plant. Within a seed is the genetic code that determines what the seed will become. An apple seed will not produce a tree that bears oranges. If the proper conditions—sun, water, and nutrients—are provided to the seed and throughout the life cycle of the young plant, there is every reason to expect that a healthy adult plant will result.

So it is with children. Each child is unique and is born with a splendid set of potentialities that will come to pass, if the proper conditions for growth are present throughout childhood.

A plant will develop specific abnormalities for each condition that is not met. Not enough water will stunt its growth; insufficient sunlight will decrease leaf and flower production; specific nutrient deficiencies will result in particular abnormalities.

When children have what they need in order to grow, the development of good character, wholesome personality, positive human relations, adequate goals, and necessary skills is *automatic*. Deviations from proper development, (emotionally and socially), can always be traced to something that has been missing in the child's experience.

The Four Conditions—What Are They?

Self-esteem is a feeling. It arises from a *sense of satisfaction* that a child experiences when certain conditions in his life have been fulfilled.

What is missing in a child's experience will always be found within one or more of the following four conditions that are required for self-esteem:

CONNECTIVENESS: *this results when a child gains satisfaction from associations that are significant to that child, and the importance of those associations has been affirmed by others.*

UNIQUENESS: *this occurs when a child can acknowledge and respect the qualities or attributes that make him or her special and different, and when that child receives respect and approval from others for those qualities.*

POWER: *this comes about through having the resources, opportunity, and capability to influence the circumstances of his or her own life in important ways.*

MODELS: *these reflect a child's ability to refer to adequate human, philosophical, and operational examples that serve to help him establish meaningful values, goals, ideals, and personal standards.*

WHAT IT MEANS TO HAVE A SENSE OF CONNECTIVENESS

For a child to have a firm sense of Connectiveness, he needs to feel:

- that he is **a part of something.** Being part of something means that the child feels he is a *functional* and important member of a family, class, gang, team, work group, etc.

- **related to other people.** Being "related" means that there are good communications, shared feelings, and a high degree of warmth and caring between the child and others.

- **identified with special groups.** By identifying, a child can label his connections (I'm a Smith, a member of the Tigers, in classroom 4-A, an American, etc.). Such labeling defines (in part) his sense of identity, and makes the *feeling* of being related specific and concrete.

- **connected to the past or a heritage.** This extends feelings of connection back in time and space. Notice how most children are enchanted with their parents' past, and stories of themselves as babies.

- that **something important belongs to him.** "Mine, mine," the young child cries. This gives way, as he grows, to object attachments, (my ball, my stereo, my car), and forms the basis for intimacy with others. Extraordinary interest in collecting and saving *things* is an expression of this need.

- that he **belongs to someone or something.** Security is enhanced when a child feels that who or what he belongs *to* will care for and protect him.

- that **the people or things that he is connected to are held in high esteem by others.** If a child's family, school, friends, object attachments, race, religion, etc. are disparaged or ridiculed, his own feelings of self worth are undermined.

- that he's **important to others.** Being important means being noticed, having one's opinions heard and considered, having one's needs weighed into decisions, and being *wanted and respected.*

- **connected to his own body,** so that he can trust it to do what he wishes. Children who are "out of touch" with their own sensory abilities, have difficulty being "in touch" with others.

The number of people or things that a child *may* feel connected to is enormous, and each person's unique experience of life gives rise to a different set. Your children may have strong feelings of connection to people or things that are not part of your experience, and vice versa.

Children need to feel connected to the important people in their lives—parents, relatives, siblings, friends, teachers, etc. A sense of Connectiveness to these people is directly related to the degree of comfort, warmth, security, understanding, humor and good will that characterizes these relationships. Anger, frustration, and poor communications undermine a child's sense of Connectiveness.

A sense of Connectiveness can also be experienced with "abstract" categories of people—even if the specific relationships are not close or intimate. A child may feel that all his classmates are important to him, though he is only a close friend of a few of them. He may know little about his teacher's personal life, but by virtue of her being his teacher, she becomes important in his life. All boys, all Black people, all football players, all Catholics, may be important sources of personal identification for a child. They may change over time, and his own fantasies, wishes, and dreams may enhance his sense of Connectiveness to them.

17

A sense of Connectiveness is enhanced or diminished by the circumstances in which a child finds himself. Different relationships become important at different times. As an example, if you have traveled in a foreign country and you could not speak the language, you probably felt close to *any* English speaking person you met, even though this connection would be totally irrelevant at home. Likewise, a child in unfamiliar circumstances will seek relationships with those he shares common characteristics with that are important *to the child at that time.* This often explains "strange" attractions that parents cannot understand.

Loyalty may be a substitute for affection in a child's relationships. Children move in and out of friendships, and often have ambivalent relationships with peers. Loyalty to groups and even institutions may over-ride a child's own frustrations and fulfill the need for a sense of Connectiveness. Example: Intense loyalty to a team on which the child is the poorest player.

Being connected goes beyond human relationships. Attachment to places and things become important elements in a child's feelings. Children often retreat to place/thing connections when human relations become problems. Any object may become a focus for feelings of connection. A hat, toy, piece of clothing, blanket, teddy bear, old pot, or piece of wood may serve to increase a child's comfort, reduce anxiety, and allow him to feel a sense of belonging. Additionally, "favorite places" may arise and disappear. Such places, his room or bed, a favorite corner, the loft, parents' bed, under the kitchen table, inside a closet, serve to activate and reinforce a child's sense of Connectiveness. All children include place/thing connections in their behavior, and they are not of lesser importance than human connections.

If a child has a broad array of person/place/thing connections that he gains satisfaction from, his self-esteem is likely to be high. Low self-esteem is characterized by a narrow range of satisfying associations. Such a narrow range gives rise to excessively dependent relationships from which a child expects all or most of his needs to be satisfied. (How these experiences come about depends on the way that significant adults arrange things. This will be dealt with in succeeding sections.)

WHAT IT MEANS TO HAVE A SENSE OF UNIQUENESS

For a child to have a firm sense of Uniqueness, he needs to have experiences that permit "differentness" to be expressed. Children with high self-esteem receive lots of support and approval for being "different" or special, and express this uniqueness in many ways. A child needs to:

- **respect himself.** He needs to value his performance, and learn to trust his perceptions. Children learn to respect and trust themselves by being respected, taken seriously, by important adults.

- **know that there's something special about himself,** even though there are many ways in which he is like others. Feeling special is something that results from how others treat him.

- **feel that he knows and can do things that no one else can.** The *way* he does things, his style or approach, often is the special characteristic of a child.

- **know that others think he's special.** He learns this through the things that people say or do to him. Being treated *as if* he's special is the basis for his individuality.

- **be able to express himself in his own way.** Being held to rigid standards of performance, without being permitted to explore alternative ways to behave, encourages a child to be inflexible and conforming.

- **use his imagination and give free reign to creative potential.** All children are naturally creative, and imaginative play is the arena in which they express themselves. If their unique, fantastic and odd expressions are disparaged, they will withdraw, and their growth will suffer.

- **enjoy being different,** while learning how *not* to make others uncomfortable. Young children will take delight in themselves, if they find parents taking delight in them. When parents can't enjoy their child's uniqueness, the child can't either.

Enhancing a child's sense of Uniqueness is not easy. There are a number of stresses associated with being "different" or "special" in our society. Striving for a sense of Uniqueness may be a natural motive in children, but we don't always make it easy for them to fulfill it.

Few parents want their children to be so different that the children risk not being accepted by their peers or other adults. Some find themselves confused as to whether they should praise a child for doing something unique for which there may not be a standard for judgment. Parents who want their children to be "good" tend to mold behavior, rather than accept expressions of individuality. Criticism seems to work better than praise in influencing behavior, at least in the short run.

Parents' own fears about being different affect the way they respond to children's uniqueness. But it's important to remember that helping a child feel special does not automatically lead to his becoming an "odd ball."

Children's need for a sense of Uniqueness is so strong that they will identify "negative" characteristics as special if their virtues haven't been acknowledged sufficiently. When a child has negative attitudes about his uniqueness, he is as tenacious in expressing those characteristics, as if he received praise for them. A child may believe that he is the worst behaved child in a class. The special role as the class "clown," or teacher hater, may prompt him to take all opportunities offered to "prove" his special position in the class. He will say or do things to create trouble, even when he knows that he will be punished for it. Excessive criticism and disapproval can lead a child to have a negative self image.

What children feel is special about themselves changes with age and the condition of their lives. Frequently children and adults do not identify the same attributes as being special. A very bright child may take his intellect for granted, seeking approval for athletic or social behavior, while adults continue to emphasize his academic accomplishments.

Everyone seeks affirmation (acceptance or approval) for what they believe is special about themselves. Children tend to be less restrained than adults. "Look at me. See what I can do!" is an expression of a child's need to have his specialness acknowledged. If a child does not receive such acknowledgement, he may "raise the ante," and behave in more and more extreme ways in order to be noticed. Chronic misbehavior is often a sign that a child's sense of Uniqueness is low.

Helping children feel special means that they are given many opportunities to express themselves (verbally, artistically, physically, playfully, and in performing their duties). They must be given positive feedback and acknowledgement that adults take pleasure in seeing such expressions of self. At the same time, they need help to *identify what it is about them that's special.*

A child may experience a sense of Uniqueness in many areas of his life. What he labels as special may result from some experience when he expressed a specific attribute or competence with considerable skill and received approval for it.

Children may feel that what makes them special is:

- what they can do with their bodies (sports, dance, etc.)
- the special skills they have (building things, organizing, etc.)
- the special talents they have (artistic, singing, academics, etc.)
- their appearance (tall, fat, pretty, ugly, etc.)
- their background (race, heritage, place of origin, etc.)
- their hobbies or interests (collecting, camping, trains, etc.)
- what they know (animals, history, special information)
- what they do (karate lessons, yell loudly, run fast, etc.)

- how they think (fantasies, imagination, humor)

- what they believe (religious beliefs, radical ideas, skepticism)

WHAT IT MEANS TO HAVE A SENSE OF POWER

Having a high sense of Power means that a child feels that he can exercise *influence* on what happens in his life. In order to have such influence, children need to learn many skills, have the opportunity to make choices, and be encouraged to take responsibility. A child needs to:

- **believe that he can usually do what he sets out to do.** This belief arises and becomes firm if a child experiences successes. Parents and teachers need to help a child be successful.

- **know that he can get what he needs in order to do what he has to do.** Children need to be provided with many resources in order to carry out their purposes. Toys, equipment, money, "junk" of all sorts need to be available.

- **feel that he is in charge of important things about his own life.** Children who are allowed to make decisions about things that are important to them develop self confidence. On the other hand, forcing children to make decisions that are beyond their capability results in a loss of a sense of Power.

- **feel comfortable when fulfilling responsibilities.** Becoming responsible starts with being given responsibilities. But the comfort that reinforces a sense of responsibility results from parents teaching needed skills, providing resources, and showing approval.

- **know how to make decisions and solve problems.** Allowing children to make decisions and teaching them effective ways to solve problems enhances their feelings of independence and personal control. Children's natural tendency to exercise such controls can be supported or undermined by parents.

- **know how to deal with pressure and stress, so as not to lose control of himself.** We can help children learn to exercise control over their feelings as well as over the external aspects of their lives without, of course, turning them into robots. If parents are too protective, it is hard for children to learn how to deal with stress.

- **use the skills he's accumulated.** Once children *can* do things, they need the *opportunity* to do them. It is especially important that children be able to use skills that are important to them. Young children often

21

obsessively do something over and over again until they are sure they know how, and then move on to something else.

Having a *sense* of Power is not the same as having power in an absolute sense. A sense of Power is the *feeling* that a child has when the above needs have been met. Being bossy, manipulating, acting spoiled, and whining so as to control others are symptoms that a child is seeking *power*, because his *sense of Power* is low.

Spoiled children have a low sense of Power, even though they appear to control many situations. If you watch a spoiled child closely, you will observe that his actions are quite predictable and patterned; he responds similarly to many events, and has little flexibility, while being manipulative. Spoiled children avoid taking responsibility, having been allowed to get others, especially parents, to take it for them. Not only will they make parents *get* them things, but their parents will make decisions for them, and do many things for them that they are capable of doing for themselves. Spoiled children do not know how to handle pressure well, and since others solve their problems for them, have not learned to solve their own. If spoiled children begin to experience the consequences of what they do, their *sense* of Power begins to grow.

Setting limits and rules adequately, providing the opportunity for children to take responsibility, and requiring children to share in duties in the home, are critical factors in helping children develop their sense of Power.

- Reasonable and clear rules provide guidelines to children so that they know what kinds of decisions they can make, and can predict parents' responses. Appropriate limits increase children's security.

- Learning to take responsibility, which includes decision making and problem solving, is the *most* important ingredient in school success. Responsible children produce rewards and praise for themselves.

- Doing chores and jobs at home requires that children learn new skills, develop organizing abilities, use skills they have, and share in important family activities. All of these add to a developing sense of Power.

WHAT IT MEANS TO HAVE A SENSE OF MODELS

Having a sense of Models results in children being able to make sense out of life. Issues that have to do with personal values, goals, and ideals reflect a child's sense of Models, as does the ability to clarify his own standards and live up to them. People, ideas and beliefs, and the child's experiences, all have an impact on the sense of Models. A child needs to:

- **know people who are worthy models for his own behavior.**
  Parents, teachers, siblings, other relatives and friends, are people whom

children learn to mimic. "Human models" are effective sources of learning when the things a child copies and uses from them result in successful experiences, e.g. copying good manners from parents.

- **grow confident in his ability to distinguish right from wrong; good from bad.** Moral and ethical standards are learned from observing, hearing what important others say, and trying them out to see whether they work. Children who hear and see a *consistent* set of standards being practiced in their families tend to adopt them.

- **have values and beliefs that are functional guides for his behavior.** Such beliefs result in actions that lead to success and reward. They also need to be aware of their own values, so as to know when to apply them. Talking about values is important. Helping a child clarify his own values and how to express them helps a child use values as a guide to behavior.

- **profit from having a broad range of experiences, so that new experiences aren't intimidating.** Every experience a child has adds to a "catalog" that serves to give him guidelines for behavior. The broader a child's experience is (those that are appropriate to age, etc.), the greater will be his confidence in facing new ones.

- **develop the ability to work toward goals, and become conscious of what they are.** Working toward goals helps a child learn emotional control, planning and problem solving, and new skills. Reaching goals (short or long range), helps children become confident in their own abilities. Example: "If you want the popsicle, you'll have to pick up your toys first."

- **make sense out of what's going on in his life.** *Excessive* change, unpredictability, conflict, emotionality, and inconsistency keep children confused. When patterns of living keep changing, a child's anxiety rises because he can't be sure that he can make accurate predictions or reach goals.

- **know the standards by which his performance, in all areas of school and home, will be evaluated.** Children are strongly motivated to please, and gain approval from, important adults. When standards are inconsistent, they can't tell whether they will receive praise or criticism for what they do. Much "misbehavior" is evidence of a child's efforts to find out what the standards are.

- **know how to go about learning.** Learning how to learn is the result of a child "organizing" his curiosity. Parents can stimulate and respond to a child's curiosity, and by doing so, help him to exercise the patience and effort required for learning.

- **have a sense of order.** By living within a relatively ordered environment, in which neatness, time commitments, and clear communication are practiced, a child develops skills in organizing, planning, and effective problem solving. Disorder in a child's environment makes it hard for him to learn good organizing tactics. This has serious consequences for school performance.

The three kinds of models that influence a child's sense of Models are:

- human models—people who are worthy of emulation

- philosophical models—ideas that guide a child's behavior and attitudes

- operational models—mental constructs and images that arise from a child's experience and determine how he handles all his activities

Whether models are "good" ones is measured by the successes or failures that children have when they put their models into practice. The ideas that a child has about the value of school, learned from parents and siblings, will influence whether a child believes school is a positive or negative experience. If a child believes the school is "good," his commitment to what he has to do there is likely to be greater, and he will tend to do better at learning tasks.

Children adopt models unconsciously, and those that influence them the most are ones that have been adopted under conditions of considerable emotional content. If a child experiences something that is associated with intense satisfaction, excitement, warmth, etc., he is likely to retain it. Likewise, things that a child experiences with intense anxiety, unhappiness or frustration are likely to be long retained, and they are often more difficult to verbalize. Yet they do influence a child's behavior. Perhaps you can recall the event(s) that influenced your own life? If so they are likely to be associated with strong feelings of one sort or another.

Two examples of the above may clarify this issue: Children who have positive early experiences with books, and whose parents receive much satisfaction from reading, tend to be motivated in reading at school; at the other end of the spectrum is the observation that parents who abuse their children tend to have been abused themselves when they were young. The models that children have, influence them when they become adults.

Once children have adopted models, it is very hard to change them. They become like information imprinted in a computer (the brain), and can only be erased or changed by considerable effort. Both teachers and parents know how much time and energy are needed to change a child's behavior; even more is required to alter feelings or attitudes. Though a pattern of behavior may result in pain or criticism, a child tends to carry out the model that he has—until he gets a new one that *he is convinced,* by his own experience, works better for him.

When children begin to associate with people outside the home, in pre-school and other places, their experience broadens, new learning occurs ("Where did they learn those dirty words?"), and they begin to develop models that parents no longer control. Folk heroes, movie stars, fantasy characters, are taken on as, albeit temporary, alternative human models. ("Who is he this week?") Television, too, has a great impact on new Models, but for most children, the effects are not usually long lasting because advertising and other distractions don't allow the experience to be intense or emotional.

Models of any sort are adopted unconsciously by children. A sense of Models is not the same as mimicry. All children do that as much more of a conscious choice. Mimicking family members, culture heroes, etc., is a device that children use to reduce anxiety, identify with a stronger or bigger person, and experiment with alternative solutions to problems.

Because modeling is unconscious, children learn more from example than from being told. This is especially important when teaching values, religious attitudes, and interpersonal behavior. Children watch, making what sense they can out of the observation, rather than fully understanding and accepting verbal messages about complex issues from parents. ("Do what I say, don't do what I do!" doesn't often work.) When parents espouse values and beliefs that a child associates with strong positive feelings, the child will tend to accept them. If parents' values are not congruent with their behavior, they don't fulfill the needs that children have. Negative feelings will be associated with many experiences, like going to church regularly for example. If children are required to attend church with the family, but find that their parents spend most of their time socializing with other adults, a child may come to feel that church going is associated with parental *disinterest* in him. Likewise, religious education, *if* it is characterized by insensitivity to children's needs, excessive pressure on children, and denial of their own uniqueness, will result in strong negative associations.

When children are in situations that they know are important to parents, but in which they experience negative or stressful feelings ("Be nice to grandpa, no matter how he acts"), they will have negative associations "imprinted" on them. In many instances, this leads to a continuing aversion to that situation, or similar ones ("Visiting Aunt Sally is just like going to Grandpa's! I have to be nice, no matter what"), and a child may either go along with it without enthusiasm, or actively reject it. If such experiences are standard family activities, such as going to church, visiting relatives, going shopping, etc., they will result in negative models, and may become philosophical principles later in life. Example: "Being too closely attached to one's family is a way of keeping one from changing."

No one of the four conditions is more important than another. Children with high self-esteem have a substantial sense of Connectiveness, Uniqueness, Power *and* Models. Low self-esteem is usually characterized by a problem in one or more of the conditions.

The material in succeeding sections will allow you to evaluate your children, and to decide which conditions need to be worked on.

III.
Having a Sense of Connectiveness: Problems and Solution

In this chapter, you will find information about the kinds of things children may do that indicate a problem in the area of Connectiveness. You will also be shown how to relate to a child so that the problems can be overcome, as well as things about a family that can increase the sense of Connectiveness of all members in it.

How Children with Connectiveness Problems Behave

First of all, a word of caution. All children will act in many of the ways described below, sometimes. One's sense of Connectiveness rises and falls, oftentimes because of changing circumstances, and, in children, some ages are less "connected" than others. What parents and teachers need to look for are:

- **Patterns** of behavior. Repeating a problem behavior, even though conditions change, is often evidence that you should take notice.

- **Intensity of expression.** When a child does some of the following things with a good deal of anger or upset feelings, he may be calling for help.

- **Number of indicators.** If a child acts in several of the ways indicated, on a continuing basis, he definitely has problems in this area.

When children have Connectiveness problems, their comfort diminishes in direct relationship to the number of people involved in a group activity. They will often make little or no effort to join in family activities, and, if large numbers of family members are present, will hang about the fringe of things without participating. Furthermore, they may voice negative attitudes about the family, and demean the accomplishments of family members, even going so far as to disparage special family characteristics, i.e. "They're all so loud;" "I don't like that kind of food;" "I hate to sing." They may set up special conditions for participating in family outings, "I'll go if I can take a friend," or make excuses for not going, "I don't feel good."

Such children will tend to spend a good deal of time by themselves, even when apparently enjoyable activities are available. A child who has shown an interest in sports may choose not to go to a ball game with a large group, thus appearing inconsistent. Being by themselves may result in focusing activities that only require one person, i.e. reading, collecting, or watching T.V.

Being reluctant to communicate is evidence of Connectiveness problems. It may be hard for parents and teachers to find out what's going on inside such a child, especially if they *try* to talk with him about what he's feeling. Low Connectiveness children tend not to volunteer much information about school or other activities. It has to be "pulled out" of them.

Friendships are terribly important to children with a low sense of Connectiveness, but they have a very ambivalent attitude toward friends. A child may have one or two friends at a time, but doesn't keep them for long. This is mainly because he or she isn't assertive in maintaining the relationship. This child may often elect to *not* play with someone who's supposed to be a friend. When a friend breaks off a relationship, such a child may try to deny that he's hurt, saying: "I don't care." These children keep their hurts to themselves, or act them out in an aggressive manner that is a "smoke screen" set up to hide their real feelings.

A low sense of Connectiveness is also indicated by a child's minimal interest in the family's racial or ethnic identification, *even though it may be important to parents*. Such general associations don't result in much satisfaction to a child, if other, more specific relationship needs remain unfulfilled.

It's easy for other children and adults to dislike a child with a low sense of Connectiveness. Such children *may not know how to relate well*. This knowledge is learned, and refined by practice. Furthermore, such children are not assertive in relationships, which gives their playmates most of the responsibility for keeping things going. When children are awkward, shy, or incompetent in human relationships, others get uncomfortable or frustrated with them. Even parents can feel uncomfortable with a child who has Connectiveness problems.

These children often appear to be "lazy," in that they don't often volunteer to help around the house, apart from regular chores they may have. They may seem to ignore the needs of other family members, but actually are avoiding doing things *with* them. Helping someone is a way of relating, and can produce anxiety in a low Connectiveness child.

These children often *seem* to relate when they're not doing so. This is frequently expressed in their interactions with adults. They may hang around, get underfoot, and interfere, but when adults try to deal with them directly, they will squirm, become silent, and appear uncomfortable and embarrassed. The same thing may occur in their relationships with other children. This behavior reflects their ambivalence—wanting to connect, but anxious about relating.

Low Connectiveness children avoid out-of-school activities that demand that they associate with others, i.e. swim classes, Little League, etc. When offered the most appealing activities, they will turn them down if the relationship requirements are substantial.

The child with a low sense of Connectiveness is *not always shy and withdrawn.* He or she may be inappropriately aggressive or demanding. But wanting people's attention is not the same as wanting to relate to them. A child who inappropriately demands such attention also turns people off, and maintains the climate in which his needs for connection are frustrated. Being loud, disparaging others, wanting to be "first," being pushy, and demanding recognition are ways of relating that the child may use, but they don't produce positive results. He may observe that people in his family relate that way, and not know how else to act. He will be jealous of others who get the limelight, at home and school.

When children act in these ways, they may get the attention they demand, but it usually produces little satisfaction, since it may involve criticism and result in punishment. Children with a low sense of Connectiveness continue to create interpersonal situations that *don't* get them what they need—warm, caring, nurturing relationships.

These children are often labeled as having a "short attention span," especially in school. Far from it! But they don't necessarily pay attention to a task; they are usually paying attention to others, or thinking about them. They watch other children relating, they fantasize about relationships, and they become anxious when related to. They are doing what they need to do, not what they're supposed to do. They're trying to deal with a low sense of Connectiveness.

And when human relationships become overly trying, as they do easily for such children, they retreat to relating to *things* rather than people. Pets, toys, objects of all sorts don't talk back, don't demand, and don't confuse. Things are easier to relate to than people. Children with Connectiveness problems may become obsessively involved in object relationships even when they're not supposed to, i.e. in class, instead of listening to the teacher. Strangely enough, their "things" provide a sense of connection, of a sort, and serve to keep their anxiety and security at a level that is acceptable. They have their favorite things, clothing, toy, etc. that they hate to be parted from; their token of relationship may be their willingness to let someone else play with a favorite object.

How to Increase a Child's Sense of Connectiveness

There are some specific ways to relate to a child with self-esteem problems that parents and teachers can employ without resorting to counseling or therapy. Not all of them will be easy but if you try them, especially ones you don't ordinarily do, you may be surprised by dramatic changes in the child who has a low sense of Connectiveness.

- **Show affection through physical contact.** Touching children is a major way to establish a sense of Connectiveness. There are lots of ways to touch a child, from a brief pat on the shoulder to a great big kissing bear-hug. It's important to know *when* and *how* a child wants or needs to be touched, but the only way to find out is to try to see his reaction. If children pull away, use brief, less demanding touches. Sometimes you will feel them "lean into" you, and then pull away;

sometimes they return the touch in kind! Parents need to respect a child's wish not to be touched, but shouldn't be fooled by apparent rejection. Everyone likes to be touched *if they are not threatened by the experience.* You can reduce threat by backing off, then continuing to initiate touching in brief, but consistent ways. Clinging children often need lots of touching, and they need to know that they don't always have to ask for it.

Many adults touch their children in a distracted manner, as if it's a bothersome thing to do. Without resorting to unnatural procedures, it is important to be conscious of a child, and let him know that you're relating to him while touching, by looking, smiling, or talking. Touching children is a way to get their attention, and for some it is an important way. Touching and getting eye contact is a way to get children to listen.

- **Show positive feelings on your face toward the child.** This may seem like a silly idea, but many parents and teachers are unaware of the effect that their facial expressions have on a child. Some smile when they're angry and frown when they're happy. Differences between what a parent or teacher says and how he looks confuse children. Smiles, or even a wink, can confirm good feeling to a child, when lots of words may not get the point across.

Eye contact increases intimacy, even if it is a bit uncomfortable for adult or child. Letting your face show anger when you feel it, makes your positive feelings more believable when they're expressed. Play a game by standing in front of a mirror with your child and experiment with different expressions that go with different emotions.

- **Tell children in words when you feel good about them.** Adults are sometimes reluctant to do this, especially if it wasn't done to them as children. It's important for children to have verbal reassurance of your positive feelings about them. It also helps them build a catalog of positive statements that they can say to others, i.e. "I love you;" "I think you're fantastic;" "You make me feel good;" etc. Teaching a child that it's o.k. to make positive statements to others by hearing them about himself improves his chances for good relationships with others—and thus his sense of Connectiveness.

- **Make praise specific.** Communicating positive feelings and giving praise are not necessarily the same. "I like your picture" is different from "You used color so nicely in this. I especially like the red and blue." Children need to know what pleases parents and teachers, and what they do well in your eyes. They need to know that what they have tried to do well has been noticed. When praise is specific it's more credible, and helps a child develop more self-awareness.

- **Let children know when you see their positive behavior having a good effect on others.** Children need to learn how to relate well. Praise for good interpersonal relations with others gives them feedback that refines their catalog of interpersonal skills. It also lets them know that human relationships are important to you. It's important that you comment on good relationships within the family, and of special importance that you let children know how they affect *you*. Comments about this should be specific, "I felt good when you didn't argue with your brother at dinner," "It makes me happy when you share what happened to you in school."

    Children who cooperate well are easily liked. Helping a child understand that cooperation is an important feature of human relationships is best done by praising him for being cooperative.

- **Share your feelings with children.** Adults have feelings that don't have anything to do with their children (really!). Children need to know that your feelings don't always result from what they do. You have bad days and good ones; nice things happen to you as well as bad; sharing some of your joys and trials makes you more human, less threatening, and a more well rounded model of good interpersonal relationships.

    Adults are sometimes afraid to share negative feelings with children for fear they will undermine a child's security or faith. But most anxiety in children is a result of not being able to make sense of what's going on. If children sense that an adult is depressed, but don't know why, they are likely to feel guilty as well as anxious. If children make you angry, telling them *why* gives them information by which they *may* change. Hidden resentments are anxiety-provoking. Letting children know that you're angry but are still "connected" to them helps them deal with angry feelings in others. Sharing your feelings helps children feel secure—the root of a positive sense of Connectiveness.

- **Share your interests, hobbies, activities, and family experiences with your children.** When your children know you better it builds their connection to you. Feeling connected to *parents* is basic to building a positive sense of Connectiveness. Knowing what *you* like builds a catalog of potential experiences for a child. Involve children in what you do (hobby, shop work, cleaning), talk to them about the way the activity makes you feel, and demonstrate how and why you do it.

    Sometimes children's involvement is distracting and intrusive. Parents want to do their own thing too! But if a child continues to put pressure on you, make a special time to expose him to the activity. He may learn and continue in it, or may have curiosity satisfied and lose interest.

- **Listen to children without judging them all the time.** This "art" is an important way to respond to children. It's done by being quiet and letting the child talk. Don't feel that you have to comment, advise, or make suggestions every time he says something. You can also paraphrase what children say, acknowledge how they're feeling ("I know how you must feel."), or encourage them to say more ("Can you tell me anything else about that?"). Asking broad general questions gives a child room to say what he wants. Some parents manipulate children by asking them very specific questions that bend the conversation into the parent's framework. That's when their kids feel that they're not being listened to. An example of this is the standard "either/or" parent question: "Did you hit your brother, yes or no?" Another alternative may be more explanatory: "Actually, Mom, it was more complicated than that. Who hit first is not clear; we both pushed and were angry at each other from yesterday." Other either/or questions imply simple moral choices that may not be so simple: "Is it right or wrong to take his cookie?" when in fact the overall situation is more complex: "He acted like I could have it, but started yelling when I ate it."

- **Do something special for children that acknowledges their special needs or interests.** Feeling that you notice and care about what he does builds a child's sense of Connectiveness. Make his favorite foods, go buy something for his hobby, get a magazine about a special interest, purchase a blouse in her favorite color—and many other small measures can communicate special attention to a child. Remember, it needs to be something that they are interested in, not what you think they ought to be interested in.

- **Avoid questioning children who are very shy.** Shy children suffer anxiety when they have to respond to questions. Making statements to them makes them feel noticed, but safe. Sometimes adults develop a habit of asking questions in order to elicit responses. When a very shy child pays attention—that is a response. If questions need to be asked, let yes or no responses suffice. As a child becomes less shy, he will elaborate more spontaneously.

Improving Relations in Your Family

Every family has a "climate" that results from the feelings, attitudes, rules, and ways of communicating that characterize the family when its members are together. Children's sense of Connectiveness is molded by the quality of interpersonal relations in the family. Family climate either enhances or diminishes its members' sense of Connectiveness.

The activities that take place when families are together reflect the degree of Connectiveness that exists. A major activity for some families is arguing, with consequent bad feelings. Other families play games and enjoy each other. All families do some of both, but a tendency toward one or the other is usual in a family.

Family climate tends to be consistent. It's based on what sociologists call "norms of behavior," unstated "rules" that guide how people interact with each other.

A norm could apply to almost anything. Some examples are:

- Children must always be reminded about chores.

- People criticize more than they praise in this family.

- Everyone uses good manners.

- People acknowledge each other when talking.

- Everyone in the family does his or her "own thing."

- People compliment each other when someone does something nice.

In order to build a sense of Connectiveness in all family members, the norms of behavior need to support positive relations among family members. What are some norms in your family? Do you have some norms that need to be changed so that better relations exist in the family? Do the norms increase or interfere with a sense of Connectiveness?

The following ideas can build better relations in your family, and enhance children's sense of Connectiveness. A word of caution is in order: if you are going to try to change the climate in your family, it will take a while for it to happen—maybe months. You can't expect everyone to "climb aboard" just because you decide to improve things, especially if Connectiveness has been low. The children will need to handle new kinds of relationships, and may not know the limits. They may not be sure that they can trust you to follow through and keep it up. Give everyone, including yourself, time to learn and adjust. In the long run you'll be glad you did.

- **Provide opportunities for family members to work and play together.** Events need to be created, coordinated, and carried out that include all family members. Make meal-times special so that everyone eats together, rather than picking up his own food. Plan a special gardening or housecleaning day, with a special event, dinner out, perhaps, to conclude it, and divide the chores up among everyone. Picnics, and family outings that everyone makes some contribution to, can be fun. Allow the kids to jump into bed with you one morning a

week, and read them stories. When it comes to special events, painting the house, buying a car, etc., let everyone voice an opinion, and consider each one seriously, even though the final decision is yours. Make one T.V. night each week special by having soft drinks and popcorn. Ask people what they would like to do as a family, and *try* to fulfill each person's wishes, including your own.

- **You can have rules that improve a sense of Connectiveness— family policies and regulations.** Rules can keep people separated: No one can go into anyone else's room. Or they can encourage good relations: If you use anything belonging to someone else you must have permission first. Having a policy that there will be a family meeting once a week can allow people to air problems and seek solutions together. Rules that apply to adults as well as kids are good: Clean the bathroom when you finish bathing. Some rules may need to be very consistently applied such as No yelling or cursing at each other; some rules imply good manners: No music after 9:00. Having some rules in the family is important—it makes children feel that the family stands for something, and introduces order and ritual into family life.

- **Increase opportunities for family members to share personal matters with each other.** If one of the children has said something important about his life to you, encourage him to tell the others at dinner. If a child develops a new interest or friend, have him let the family know about it, at meal-time or a family meeting. If one parent works late or odd hours, be sure to have a special meal from time to time, so that parent is included. Parents take the lead and act as models by sharing things from their lives that children don't know about. What happened at work or on trips can be interesting to children. Stories from parents' past are always winners. *It's not the content that is always important; it's the parents' willingness to share themselves that sets a tone, especially if feelings are discussed as well as events. Listen non-judgmentally to children's concerns and feelings—they will be encouraged to share more often.*

- **Improve clarity about people's "roles" in the family.** This mainly has to do with responsibilities and chores, insuring that everyone has some responsibilities that they fulfill consistently. Who does what, when, in your family? Is the distribution of responsibilities fair? Do they change periodically to meet personal and family changes? Who makes what decisions? It's important to adjust roles when circumstances require. If Mom takes a job, other family members may have to take over some of her duties. Chore lists for all members of the family may help. What are the responsibilities that children in the family have for each other, especially younger siblings, and what are the limits to those responsibilities? Sometimes family members are given "negative roles"—the clown, the failure, the hard-nosed parent, the soft touch, the bad kid. When such roles become fixed, it's hard for that person to act in other ways. Talk about such roles, and see what everyone, including the person so labeled, can do to create new roles.

- **Foster the positive solution of interpersonal problems among family members.** Unresolved conflicts between parents, between children, or among parents and children destroy a sense of Connectiveness in the family. Some mechanism such as family council or a rule about taking time to talk about a conflict can help. Emphasizing problem solving rather than seeking fault can be an important norm in the family. Rules and limits about conflicts and resolving them are necessary, even though not everyone is completely satisfied by them. Simple rules and consequences about excessive arguing or fighting often help to reduce the quantity of conflict in a family. Give children a time and place to talk things out, often right on the spot, without always providing them with a solution. Encourage them to find a solution within reasonable limits that you set. (Smashing each other in the face is not reasonable.) Parents act as a model for handling conflicts. When they can't handle ones that they have, it's hard for children to do better.

IV.

Having a Sense of Uniqueness: Problems and Solutions

In this chapter you will find information about the kinds of things children may do that indicate a problem in the area of Uniqueness. You will also be shown how to relate to a child so that the problems can be overcome, as well as things a family can do to increase the sense of Uniqueness of all of its members.

How Children with Uniqueness Problems Behave

As indicated at the beginning of Chapter III, (page 27), it's important to remember that all children show these problem behaviors sometimes. As an observer, you should look for *patterns* (behavior that is repeated in different situations), intensity (behavior associated with a good deal of emotion), and the *number of behaviors* that indicate that a child has a low sense of Uniqueness.

Children who have a low sense of Uniqueness tend to place restrictions on their imagination. They don't seem to enjoy making up fanciful stories, and they feel safest with repetitive play, because they are uncomfortable with change. A child with a low sense of Uniqueness doesn't seem to enjoy word games, puns, or subtle jokes, and rarely tells them. They usually tell poor lies, and generally mimic what others do, rather than creating their own fantasies. They need to be told precisely how to do things, rarely using their own creativity to fill in gaps, and don't have a distinctive way in which they go about things.

Children with Uniqueness problems may *show-off* a lot, but it will usually be inappropriate. Their showing off will not vary much from situation to situation. Young children (toddlers), love to show off a lot, which is necessary if they are to develop a sense of Uniqueness. If they receive acknowledgement and approval for it at that stage, they usually don't have to do it so much when they get to be school age. Actually, low uniqueness children are seeking recognition and praise which they have *not* gotten, and in spite of criticism or even punishment, will persevere in inappropriate, show-off behavior.

Paradoxically, such children will retreat when singled out, or called upon in school, but will show off when others are the center of attention, or when others are engaged in some creative activity. Adults are inclined to tell such a child to "put up or shut up." Also much of the show-off behavior is "regressive;" it would be appropriate to a younger child, but not for one that age.

A child with Uniqueness problems rarely or never contributes original ideas. He tends not to have a unique way of looking at things and will usually repeat other's ideas, even in the same discussion, especially those of children or adults he feels are special. Characteristically, he will not have many ideas to contribute to resolving a problem in the family, and tends to be satisfied with the commonplace rather than the unusual.

Such a child will want to go to the usual places, and rarely wants to see new sights or to try new kinds of activities. He seldom has much curiosity about a new topic that is discussed by the family, and will not ask questions or seek new ideas.

A child with a low sense of Uniqueness **conforms to the wishes and ideas of other** children or adults. Wearing what others wear, doing what others do, and saying what others say is characteristic of the low Uniqueness child. He often will appear to be easily led, and will not assume much leadership unless he can check with others for approval. Not being able to elicit the attention he seeks, for example, if parents or teachers are busy, will make this child uncomfortable and anxious.

Children with a low sense of Uniqueness become easily embarrassed and apologetic if it's pointed out to them that they are doing or saying something that is different from others. Public praise "Everybody, look at what Jane is doing!" is hard for these children to accept. It sets them apart, and only as their sense of Uniqueness rises can they begin to take delight or pride in their own unique accomplishments.

Associated with this is the tendency to disparage their own performance: "I don't think that's very good." This should not be confused with humility. The low Uniqueness child really is not convinced that much of what he does is very special, and it's almost impossible to convince him that it is.

These children tend to have a narrow range of emotional expression. They rarely express spontaneous joy or elation, and similarly don't get terribly sad or depressed. They appear to be un-selfconscious, not reflecting on or evaluating their own behavior or feelings, rather tending to repeat what others say about themselves, "Yes, I'm sad too, like Jimmy."

How to Increase a Child's Sense of Uniqueness

There are ways to relate to a child that can have a positive impact on his sense of Uniqueness, without letting him "get away" with everything. Having a sense of Uniqueness—a positive feeling of individuality—does not mean that a child must become spoiled, uncontrollable, or so "different" that he no longer conforms to ordinary limits. Feeling "special" does not mean feeling "better" than others, or that a child need be excused from normal social conventions.

- **Encourage children to express ideas that may be different from your own.** Even if you don't agree with them, they need to know you respect their ideas. This is especially important when helping children solve problems. A child profits from knowing that he can express ideas, even if they are "weird," and if parents don't get upset by them, they usually dissolve because they don't work as solutions.

- **It's important to communicate acceptance to children.** This communication is done by giving verbal recognition to a child's feelings, attitudes, and opinions. Even though limits need to be set and adhered to, acceptance and recognition can be voiced: "I understand why you did that, but I can't allow it." You need to have some sense of why a child has done something. The art of "accepting the child but not the deed" is expressed through appropriate communications. Understanding and accepting do not mean that you must become more permissive.

- **Point out how something about a child is different or special.** Other children may possess the same quality, but each child feels special about himself. Expressing something in his own way is what makes a child special *to himself*. It's this *recognition* of the child that's important. Pointing out such things as "You dance divinely;" "You paint such colorful pictures;" "You were especially nice when Aunt Jane was here," give a child a frame-of-reference and labels for his own specialness. In addition, it helps a child when positive changes are pointed out: "You weren't able to climb that the last time we were here. You are sure getting better at it."

It's especially important to let your child know that it's o.k. to not have the same opinion that others do—the same likes and dislikes. Being different from others should not undermine a child's acceptability.

- **Allow children to do things their own way, as much as possible,** stopping short of offending others or intruding on their rights. If you set a task for a child, let him complete it, within appropriate time limits, and to acceptable standards, in his own way. When you give approval to children for doing a job in a unique way, their sense of Uniqueness is raised. You can allow them to make decisions about how they organize their toys, which ones are most valued, how to decorate their rooms, what colors they like, etc.

- **Increase opportunities for children to express themselves creatively.** You should have lots of materials available at home so that a child can easily find different ways to express himself: crayons, paints, different kinds of paper, wood scraps, pencils, etc. Play music and encourage children to dance to it; have a child make up a story with you; make common, everyday tasks into fanciful games. Imagination is a substitute for wealth when it comes to providing children with creative play objects. Simple toys that allow a child to create fantasies with them are important. Discarded household items can become valued playthings.

- **Allow children lots of time to express their special interests in creative ways.** Don't be concerned that a child seems to be compulsive about one activity. Children's interests change over time, even though they deeply immerse themselves in one kind of activity for quite awhile. They often like to use space in creative ways, i.e. making a cabin under the kitchen table. Children with a high sense of Uniqueness tend to see creative opportunities in the most ordinary places or things. Costumes, old discarded clothes, can permit a child to extend a creative interest. Library books can enhance their involvement in a subject. Listen to the stories they tell about what they're doing. Some early childhood "obsessions" become life-long interests for some people. Don't disparage special interests.

- **Avoid ridiculing or shaming children,** even though you may have to place limits on their activities. Ridicule tells a child that he has made a poor choice about how to express himself. Fear of ridicule encourages a child to hold back from expressing himself. Shaming a child implies that he is being judged against some other standard, making him feel that his own unique approach is not respected. When placing limits on children, you should emphasize that what he's doing, not his character or personality, is at issue.

- **Help children find acceptable ways to express themselves.** It is usually not *what* a child is doing that is punishable, but rather *how* or *where* he's doing it. A child playing loudly in his room may be o.k., but not in the midst of mother's tea party. Painting may be acceptable at the kitchen table, but not on the living room sofa. Playing quietly in the family room may be tolerable, but not with a lot of noise. Help children find ways to carry on their activities so that they don't interfere with others. This increases their awareness of the effect they have. When a child "does his thing," it doesn't mean that others must stop doing theirs. Children can be oblivious to their surroundings, including other people, when they get deeply into fanciful play. Tolerance and patience are required. Being creative does not mean that a child has to be obnoxious. When you offer a positive alternative to something being done inappropriately, and the alternative is used, reinforce it with praise and recognition.

- **When children have a low sense of Uniqueness, use private praise.** Public praise that is overly enthusiastic, even within the family, tends to embarrass children with Uniqueness problems. Reviewing their positive accomplishments of the day at bedtime is a useful tactic. Drawing them aside to whisper praise in their ear, makes it very special.

Encouraging Individuality in Your Family

As we pointed out in Chapter III, (page 33), children's self-esteem reflects the "family climate," which is determined by the "norms of behavior." A family can have an atmosphere that encourages a sense of Uniqueness in children. In order to do so, the following material should be carefully considered.

One of the most important issues in enhancing a sense of Uniqueness in family members has to do with the *"norms" about individuality* in the family. How much diversity is allowable in your family? Does everyone have to do things in the same way? Can members of the family be different from one another without being ridiculed or criticized? When members of a family are respected for their own unique style in expressing ideas, feelings, and opinions, a climate that encourages a sense of Uniqueness is present. Enforcing limits does not interfere with this—there need to be rules about *how* people relate and express themselves, without censoring what they say, i.e. no put-downs or criticism of each other at dinner.

Physical arrangements can influence the sense of Uniqueness. Each member of the family needs some private space, or special places, such as shelves, cupboards, or furniture. Children who must share rooms needn't have to share everything in the room. People who have their own rooms

45

should have a major influence on how it's decorated or arranged. Rules that protect privacy and, especially, personal belongings need to be clarified.

It should be pointed out that encouraging a sense of Uniqueness in the family has its price. Respecting individuality may mean that things become a bit disorganized at times. Not everyone will be moving in the same direction at the same time. Encouraging creative expression may make the place somewhat messy. If order, neatness, and "togetherness" are too rigidly adhered to, encouraging Uniqueness will suffer, and vice versa. Parents must find their own most tolerable balance. If parents need to control everything, then building a sense of Uniqueness will suffer. It depends on how different from yourself you are willing to allow your children to be.

"The Family" and its needs should not be used as a method for making children feel guilty and controlling their behavior. Each individual in the family does and should have an impact on the way things happen in the family. Sometimes the needs of an individual must take precedence over family activities. If a child has had a special disappointment or upset, dinner or bedtime might be altered to take his feelings into consideration. Enhancing a sense of Uniqueness encourages individuals to depart from usual patterns. A child or parent may become deeply involved in some project or task that, for example, justifies exempting him or her from a family outing.

Providing **incentives for good performance needs to be emphasized,** rather than punishment for poor performance. Even though limits and rules may require punishing children from time to time, children need to receive rewards in order to recognize their own positive performances. Rewards should be individualized, as much as possible, so that they are consistent with each child's special interests or values. Surprising children with unexpected rewards lets them know that their special efforts have been recognized and appreciated. Encourage children to use special skills or talents by giving them praise and rewards for doing so.

Consider children's special skills, talents or interests when you assign duties or chores. When children are well trained and knowledgeable about how to do their tasks, they will be more likely to complete them successfully. Knowing that they can do some things surpassingly well increases children's sense of Uniqueness. Some parents go so far as to carefully teach a child how to start a car on a winter morning, so that it's warmed up when Dad has to go off to work. A child may have a special recipe that he prepares well—let him provide it for the family from time to time. All of this applies to all family members, including parents. Even Mom and Dad have their special things they like to do. Provide recognition for them.

Even rules have to be broken when unpredicted circumstances arise. Slavishly following rules in the face of unanticipated events denies the unique needs of family members. Breaking a rule from time to time does not mean that the rule is irrelevant, if you clearly communicate that the circumstances are special. Too many special circumstances, though, can create a great deal of confusion. Being flexible does not mean being "wishy-washy." The process of enhancing Uniqueness is a special skill that parents and teachers have to work on. Keep in mind that rules that are reasonable and appropriate can be followed most of the time, and departure from them need not be chaotic.

We would be doing you a disservice if we were to suggest that enhancing a child's uniqueness is easy. It requires considerable clarity, flexibility, and patience from parents. In the long run, children profit enormously from the efforts to do so. A child's self-esteem is based on a comfortable sense of individuality.

V.
Having a Sense of Power: Problems and Solutions

In this chapter the issues that have to do with children's sense of Power will be explored. Problems in developing a sense of Power, how to relate to children so as to increase it, and how the family can become a place where everyone's sense of Power is enhanced will be explained.

How Children with Power Problems Behave

Again, we wish to caution you that all children show these problem behaviors sometimes.

Children who have a low sense of Power are often *stubborn and "bossy."* They insist on having things their way, even though what they want may be unreasonable. They may try to boss older siblings, as well as parents. It's hard to convince them that there are better alternatives to a problem than what they're doing. Even though such a child will be stubborn and bossy in many situations, he also will *avoid taking responsibility for others.* He may try to tell siblings what to do, but when he has to take care of them the situation will rapidly deteriorate into arguing. Being bossy is contrary to being able to get along with others well. Such a child will, if accepted by peers, tend to be a follower rather than leader, even though he may try to boss them around.

Such children frequently *act helpless* and *give up easily* in the face of mild frustration. They don't handle frustration well at all. By giving up and acting helpless they force others to take responsibility. Actually, being helpless is a way of asserting power, in that it makes others do something for a child. It results in a "low" feeling of power, but without the feeling of satisfaction that children with a high sense of Power experience. These children will use almost any excuse to justify giving up: pains and aches, "it's unimportant," pleading ignorance, doing it "later," etc. This characteristic is continually frustrating to parents and teachers who know that the child *does* have the capability to do something. A poor sense of Power interferes with a child using what he knows.

Often a child who has a low sense of Power *is physically awkward and incompetent*. He will have difficulty in strenuous athletic activities, and try to avoid taking physical risks, that his peers perform quite comfortably, such as climbing, balancing, etc. Such children tend to stumble, drop things and bump into objects as if they are out of touch with their bodies. This characteristic results from anxiety that produces tensions in a child's body, so that he cannot be as graceful or adept as peers with high self-esteem.

In general, children with low sense of Power *avoid taking responsibility*. When given tasks to perform they will forget to do them, dawdle over simple ones, make excuses, or leave the scene. This lack of responsibility extends to their own selves. Getting dressed, rising on time, remembering things they want to do, and meeting conditions that are required for getting something they want, become problems. These children are called "spoiled." By avoiding responsibility they invariably put others in a position where they have to take it for them. Teachers give them extra help, parents "do it" instead of the child. While spoiled children who appear to be getting away with a lot seem to profit from their irresponsibility, they actually miss many opportunities for satisfaction because of their low sense of Power.

Low Power children *don't exercise initiative*. They wait for others to take charge or start things. They get bored easily, but, nevertheless, wait for others to take the lead in doing things. Even then, they will drag their feet, especially if the suggestion requires some effort. They need to be reminded about chores, and kept at them until they finish. Even in activities that they enjoy, these characteristics are evident. They often don't do the simplest things required to accomplish something, such as calling a friend when they need a playmate.

These children *avoid challenges*, even in simple tasks, and act helpless in the face of anything that *they themselves perceive* as challenging. Even though parents may know, beyond a doubt, that a child is capable of doing something, it's the child's own assessment that influences his behavior. This leads to conflicts, when a parent feels that a child is lazy. Actually, the child may fear failure more than parents' wrath.

A low sense of Power is usually associated with *poor emotional control*. This is manifested by excessive crying, anger, or depressions that a child cannot lift himself out of without depending on others to make him feel good. A low Power child will often react to apparently unimportant events with a great show of emotion, and parents are left wondering what it was all about. This latter occurs because a low Power child tends to be unaware of why he's reacting or what it is he's reacting to. This isn't a game. His excessive crying or anger is a result of his low sense of Power which he can't report, not the event that seemed to cause the outburst.

Children with a low sense of Power attempt to compensate for it by *trying to gain power over others*. They may like to direct and lead, and have their own way. But they are invariably poor at it, interfering with the rights and needs of others. They will blindly insist that they know the "right" way to do something, and will get depressed when their way fails or is not accepted by others. They are manipulative—a sign that they can't get what they want in more appropriate ways.

Children's low sense of Power is generally based on *poor skills and incompetence in many areas*. Having a low sense of Power results in a vicious circle. Poor skills result in excessive failure in what he tries to do. Failure promotes and reinforces a sense of powerlessness. This, then, makes a child reluctant to accept challenges and risks, and take the responsibility and initiative that are required for learning. Most children who have difficulty learning lack a sense of Power. They have a hard time with any kind of learning, even when they repeat some process over and over again. Only when their sense of Power begins to rise can they begin to learn effectively.

How to Increase a Child's Sense of Power

Building children's sense of Power is another important foundation stone for their self-esteem. It is important to keep in mind that a sense of Power is a *feeling;* one that permits a child to be confident when doing things he has to do. Having control over others, being manipulative and domineering are *not* the goals of this condition.

- **Make sure that children are confronted with issues of personal responsibility.** A sense of personal responsibility grows over time, and most of us are still learning about it long into adulthood. But if children are started early on this road, the transition to adulthood is easier. Being responsible means that a child is aware that his own actions contributed to the outcome of some event, and that what he does makes a difference.

  It's important that you let children know when they have been irresponsible *and* when they have acted responsibly. Confronting or reminding children about being responsible does not necessarily mean

51

punishing them. Letting them know that responsibility is an important issue to you begins to build their awareness.[1]

- **Provide alternatives when planning activities,** so that children have choices to make. Making choices and acting on them is an exercise of the sense of Power, and parents can help children develop it, in everyday activities ("Would you like a peanut butter or tunafish sandwich for lunch?"), and larger issues ("On Saturday we can go to the beach or the amusement park. Where would you like to go?"). When children balk at doing something, giving them alternatives can often remove the block, "Well, you have to take a bath but you can have it with bubbles or without. Which do you prefer?" Increase opportunities for children to make choices about personal matters such as clothing, food, toys, room arrangement, books and games. You can always let them make choices in areas that are of minor concern to you.

- **Let children know that they are responsible for what they feel.** Children tend to react impulsively and emotionally to many situations. One characteristic of maturity is that a person has some control over his reactions to things. Children blame people, events, fate, or anything else for the way they feel. Blaming excessively is a symptom of a low sense of Power. Learning to take responsibility for and control of feelings is another lifelong issue, but children can be helped to learn about how to express their feelings appropriately. A child who can exercise self restraint has an enormous advantage in dealing with situations that might provoke anger, fear, resentment, or frustration.

- **Teach children how they can influence people in a positive way.** Having effective skills in human relations allows children to get what they want without upsetting other people. Children are not born knowing how to relate well; they must learn it. They chiefly do so by watching others, especially parents and teachers, relate. Simple good manners, learned and reinforced on a day-to-day basis, are actually the most useful basis for good relationship skills. "Please," "Thank you," and "May I" are simple and easy places to start. Waiting one's turn, not interrupting, and making others comfortable can be taught to youngsters, especially by insisting that they deal with *you* in these ways: "I'm on the phone now, but will talk to you as soon as I am finished."

- **Help children be aware of how they make decisions.** The ability to make decisions comfortably is the key to a sense of Power. Children make decisions all the time, but are usually unaware of the process, i.e. weighing alternatives, foreseeing consequences, making choices based on values. Decision making is a skill that is refined by practice and self consciousness. When children do something, for good or ill, you can point out that what happened was the result of a decision. You can discuss impending decisions with them. You can review good and bad decisions, so that they have reference points for the future. You can even face them with making decisions about their feelings: "I'd like you to decide whether you're going to get angry every time your sister does that to you. If you don't want to, I'll help you think through another way to handle it."

- **Teach children better ways to solve problems,** and be sure that they have problems to solve. One trap that parents fall into is giving their children too much help in solving problems, doing it for them. You can *provide* a solution for a problem, or you can help a child *think through* the solution himself. When a child has a problem, don't immediately give advice, but offer him help by asking questions about the problem: "I know that math problem is hard. But look at the one you just did. Is there a clue in that one?" Children's sense of Power rises dramatically when they realize that they have solved a knotty problem themselves. Children will ask adults to solve problems for them constantly. Even though, in the short run, it may seem more "efficient," time-wise, to give them a solution, in the long run encouraging their own sense of Power will be more productive.

- **Plan activities so that a child's chances of experiencing success are increased.** Experiencing success is the source of high self-esteem. When you have a child do something, a chore, solve a problem, or any complex operation, the best course is to break down the activity into steps so that he can complete one stage at a time, successfully. Parents frequently ask children to do very complex things like cleaning their rooms without providing a step-wise plan for doing it. When children get lost in the midst of a complicated activity, they tend to give up, with a loss in their sense of Power. Teaching children how to do things well, by words *and* by example, increases their chances for success. In addition, parents need to provide any resources that a child might need to perform an activity, especially if the child is not aware of what resources are available, e.g. give him a treated cloth rather than a dry rag to dust his room.

53

- **When children show that they can do something well, allow them to do it.** A sense of Power is reinforced by having the opportunity to do the things we do well. Children take pride in their skills, just as adults do. If a child shows a talent and interest in cooking, let him do it as often as is reasonable. If a child reads well and enjoys it, let him have the time and place to do it—pointing out in the process how it is a special skill. Most children do *something* that they identify as a special skill. It's important that parents make space for it. Example: even a toddler can be a good "helper" at the supermarket.

- **Help children set limits for themselves and others.** You can demonstrate this by setting clear and consistent limits yourself. This doesn't only mean having rules. It has to do with personal limits such as "I will not give you what you want when you speak to me in that tone of voice," and "I told you that I would take you shopping if you were home on time. Since you were late, I'm not obliged to take you. We'll have to plan another time." Living within firm limits gives a child a "sense of limits," and teaches him to use self-restraint. Setting limits for children allows them to know what kinds of decisions they can make, and to predict the consequences of their actions.[2] Help children to say "no" to things that may not be good for them to do. Children need help to set limits with their peers: "If Joey asks you to give him answers in class, I think it's o.k. if you don't. Try it, see what happens, and we can talk about it again." They also may need continuing support to say no in personal matters: "You don't have to let your sister borrow your clothes. I'll support you in that."

Reducing Conflict in the Family

Power within the family is an issue that is usually associated with conflict. "Power struggles" between parents, or among parents and children are evidence that the family climate does not enhance a sense of Power in each of its members. When people have a high sense of Power they have less need to "win," because they are already confident that their opinions and contributions to the family can make a difference. There are a number of things that a family can do that serve to increase the sense of Power of children, without giving them power that they're unable to handle wisely.

Many of the issues having to do with power relate to the way conflict is handled. When conflicts are resolved by having "winners" and "losers" it usually results in conflict returning quickly. No one likes to be a loser. The pattern is usually set by parents. If they always have to be winners, it then follows that children have to be losers. If parents are willing to negotiate some things with children, discuss differences reasonably, try to clarify opinions and feelings, then children see that there is opportunity to influence the parents. If, as a result of these procedures a parent "gives in" or changes an opinion, then children's ability to give in is also enhanced. Parents don't have to win in every confrontation with children in order to gain their respect. Clarity, reasonableness, fairness, consistency, and concern are more likely to result in children respecting parents than using the "club" of parental authority—not that it isn't required sometimes, but probably less than parents think. When parents can admit mistakes, apologize, and change, it increases children's faith in them, enhances feelings of security, and results in children's sense of Power increasing.

Parents should **avoid altering rules and procedures without discussion or prior warning.** Being arbitrary, which means using parental authority in unpredictable ways, robs children of a sense of Power. It's also usually a sign that parents are resentful and frustrated, more often than not as a result of being unclear with children in the first place. Children need to feel that they can influence the rules under which they live. When parents act arbitrarily they erase any rights that children may have. Children's sense of Power is increased when they can plan some of their own activities. When parents act arbitrarily, with unpredicted demands, children's ability to plan successfully is undermined.

Family members should be involved in significant decisions that affect them. It is useful to ask children what kind of rules they believe are needed, and what chores they have a preference for. This does not mean that everything they say needs to be done, but it does show that their opinions are taken into consideration. All family members should have the opportunity to indicate preferences about family matters. Family outings, vacations, picnics, etc., are splendid opportunities for children to have a say in what happens. When children know that they *can* influence decisions, they are usually more accepting of those that parents make. Knowing that they can have an affect means their sense of Power is high; under these conditions their *need to control* diminishes.

Allowing children to influence decisions doesn't mean putting everything to a vote, where parents only have one vote apiece. Voting sometimes, though, when parents don't have a strong vested interest, is a useful exercise in family democracy. The kind of "family democracy" we mean is one in which members are heard and respected, even though parents are in charge.

In order to build a sense of Power in the family, **there need to be ways to deal with grievances.** Grievances are those chronic issues that we often come to accept: "You'll just have to live with it, that's the way Dad is;" "She never puts the top back on the toothpaste;" "I can't stop her from wearing your socks." Sometimes it's important to isolate grievances by having only the parties involved discuss them. Sometimes parents have to step in, as in controlling younger children from tormenting older ones. Sometimes issues need to be aired in a family meeting where everyone can voice an opinion. There are some grievances that can't be "solved," but may be tempered by being able to talk about them openly. When grievances are disregarded or suppressed, family members feel that they cannot control their own lives, and their sense of Power diminishes.

By being aware of increasing capabilities and skills in children, parents should **encourage them to take on more challenging tasks and responsibilities.** Children, like adults, are creatures of habit, often being satisfied to stick with what they can do well. With parental encouragement, they may find they have greater potentialities than they thought: "I'm sure you can go down the slide by yourself. Try it, and you'll see." As a child becomes aware that he grows and changes, his willingness to try new activities increases his sense of Power. Often this means that parents need to lead children into taking greater risks, without demanding that they go beyond what they feel comfortable with. Parents' support and encouragement is often enough to encourage a child to try something new.

In families this should result in older children not only having greater responsibilities, but also more privileges than younger ones. Children need to know that they can gain more of what they want through increased competence and responsibility, and this should be spelled out as directly as possible: "Since you've done all your chores without any hassle for some time now, I think that we can allow you to stay up later. You've shown that you can be responsible." Often, children seek new privileges. Whether they get them or not can be related to their demonstrating growth in responsibility: "If you wish to be able to ride down to the store alone on your bike, you'll have to show me that you can be home on time, or call me if you can't."

The resources that families have need to be distributed to family members in a fair and equitable way. Money, for allowances or payment for services, is an important resource. But money is not the only category of resources that a family has. Space and time are equally important. As an example, older children may need special resources because of their particular responsibilities. Space for privacy, quiet places to do homework, special things such as desk lamps, books, party clothes, etc., are needed more by older children than younger ones. Parents' time and energy are also resources in the family, and children often fight and argue over these resources. If parents give some special time each week to individual children, it gives each one the feeling that he or she has some influence over this valued resource. But parents need to spend time with each other in order to have some sense of control, and single parents need to have special time with other adults. Controlling this special resource—time—is a never-ending challenge, and demands that some structure and order be placed on activities.

When parents allocate special time, the impact on a child's sense of Power is profound, especially if it is consistent and predictable. Fifteen minutes every day or two spent alone with a child, when the child can select any activity that is reasonable, a story, game, or just talking, builds trust and a child's sense of Power. This time needs to be sacred, and neither other obligations nor any punishment the child is under should interfere with it. Spending all or part of a day from time to time with individual children builds further on this.

Using resources effectively also suggests that they not be squandered by giving children too much without some corresponding evidence of responsibility on the children's part. When children know what resources they can get, *through the efforts they make,* their sense of Power is enhanced.

The sense of Power and sense of responsibility are very closely associated. You help children grow in a sense of responsibility **when you are clear about what they are responsible for, and what decisions they can make on their own.** A problem area in most families is the way older children take responsibility for younger ones. The older ones are often given the responsibility, but have little authority to control the younger ones. This creates a paradox. Responsibility and authority are separated, and that leads to strife and bad feelings.

When a child has the responsibility for some duty, he or she should have broad latitude in deciding how to do it, if standards and time limits have been clarified: "I don't care how you do your room, as long as it's done by 3:00 and is clean." Giving children lots of chores, but not allowing them to have a say in them does *not* build a sense of Power.

In order to accomplish all of this in a reasonable manner, parents need to be very clear, in their own minds, over what areas they need to maintain control, and what decisions they are willing to let children make. *Doing the "right" thing* is less important than being clear about what you're doing and why, so that children can understand.

VI.
Having a Sense of Models: Problems and Solutions

In this chapter the issues that have to do with children's sense of Models will be discussed. How do children who have problems with their sense of Models act and how can you relate to them to enhance their sense of Models? The family issues that bear on this condition will be described.

How Children with Models Problems Behave

All children have problems with their Models. This is because they are continually learning, refining what they know, changing, and having new experiences. The nature of childhood is always to be a bit confused. Therefore, everything we describe below about problems with a sense of Models, actually applies to all children. But a child has a severe problem in this area when he demonstrates many of these behaviors in *most* situations, and is, therefore, severely handicapped by excessive tension and anxiety.

Chronic confusion is a major symptom of children with Models problems. They have difficulties carrying out even the simplest instructions and appear to become disinterested in most tasks very quickly, even those in which they have stated some interest. Keeping them "on target" is often akin to trying to hold mercury in your hand. This characteristic is the result of a deeper problem that such children have, which is a general absence of a "goal orientation."

When children have a sense of goals, it means that they have some model of where they're headed in a particular task, and some notion of how to get there. Children with Models problems usually don't. They will often "waste" time in apparently aimless activity, or may become involved in some peripheral activity that doesn't lead them toward the goal at hand. A confusion results between the goals they have agreed on ("I'll put my books away."), your goals for them ("I want you to, so your room can be cleaned."), and short term, impulsive goals ("Why are you playing with the dog when you're supposed to be putting your books on the shelf?"). Even though they often appear to be busy, children with Models problems will move from one activity to another, and not wind up at any place close to where they initially headed. The lack of clear goal orientation will also show up in the way such a child reports about what he's doing. He will have a great deal of difficulty conceptualizing or discussing goals. When asked to specify the purpose of an activity, even if he has been told what it is, he will give vague or inaccurate answers, as if he doesn't have a clue why he's doing it.

Children with Models problems *get confused easily,* even about ordinary matters. Such things as when some *regular* task is to be done, where the family is going next weekend, what time dinner is served, when special events happen—all get mixed up. In a child with a low sense of Models this is not avoidance or manipulativeness, and is often associated with depression or anxiety about not being able to keep things straight. Such tendency toward confusion should also not be labeled as low intelligence, since it isn't. It only points up the degree to which what we call intelligence depends on the ability to organize and work towards goals.

When children have a low sense of Models, **they tend to be quite disorganized, sloppy and messy.** When their spaces, rooms, desks at school become disaster areas, and they are required to straighten them, they frequently take an exceedingly long time to do so and still not have them organized in any logical manner. In matters of dress and personal hygiene they will be found wanting, but tend to mimic parent's standards in this area. They will leave tops off of jars, tools lying around, not pick up after themselves, and in general leave a trail of unfinished business as they wander from activity to activity. Yelling and screaming doesn't seem to make any inroads on this characteristic. Unfortunately, they may become labeled as the stereotyped "absent-minded professor," and parents resign themselves to the problem.

These children have a hard time making decisions because of the lack of an organizing principle or sense of direction. They will pick out peripheral or unimportant elements of a situation to be concerned about rather than the most important factors: "You've spent a half hour straightening out your hairpins, but the rest of the job isn't going to get done on time." Since we make decisions, always, in terms of some goal that we have, low Models children tend to avoid making them. Their decisions tend not to lead anywhere, and thus the result of decision making for them is unrewarding. Their difficulty in making decisions even affects the way they communicate. They often can't decide what they want to say or how to say it; they tend to start sentences, but not complete them and start ideas but not finish them. When asked simple questions, they will shrug, stare blankly at you, or ask you what you mean.

Sometimes children with a low sense of Models **become obsessive in insisting that there is only one way to do something.** Once they have discovered a method that works in dealing with a situation or task, they will tend to hold on to it, even applying it at times when it is not totally appropriate. They will usually not generalize, diversify, or embellish the solution, or be creative in altering it. Moreover, they will often insist that others follow the same solution or have the same idea, and will become angry and frustrated if others don't. As a result of this characteristic, if their solution doesn't work, as is often the case, they will give up rather than seek an alternative.

This obsessive rigidity extends to the standards that they hold to. When they get an idea in their heads, it's hard for them to change. If something's right, it's *always* right; if wrong, *always* wrong. Changing results in anxiety. Rigidly held standards are like a life raft to which they hold, even though a rescuer is nearby. Children with Models problems *have a low tolerance for ambiguity.* When things become unclear, they become anxious, and retreat to rigidity, or leave the scene.

Since they have difficulty sizing up a situation in terms of goals, they can't make good choices about what's important; they can't let something go and get on with another piece of the puzzle. They often become excessively concerned with time, and can't shift schedules easily. Work piles up on them because they can't select the most important thing to do on the basis of priorities that will move them toward a goal. They often demand unrealistic perfection of themselves and others, and, in doing so, insure their own failure or interpersonal problems with others.

The whole area of **ethics and morals is a problem for children** with a low sense of Models. Making consistent ethical choices involves a basic set of beliefs (philosophical models) that act as a reference point for decisions. Since these children tend to be unsure about what it is they believe, their decisions about truth/falsity, right/wrong, and good/bad tend to be contradictory and inconsistent. They may voice high moral beliefs, but their behavior doesn't correspond to them. They will be confused about the right or wrong way to handle a situation. There is a general lack of integration or coherence to their beliefs and the way they're put into practice. They will often be accused of lying or being hypocritical, but will not understand why.

They often really *can't* tell what is true and what isn't, and may get events so confused in their own minds, that they truly believe that "black is white."

Children with Models problems **tend to shy away from new experiences** for several reasons. One is because their own experience is probably limited—that's one reason why they have a low sense of Models. Secondly, new experiences are only chosen if they make sense in terms of some goal we have. These children's problems with goals often diminish their enthusiasm for new experiences.

Children who have a low sense of Models may become "chameleons" around people. Having little sense of an integrated self, they may mimic whomever becomes important to them, peers or adults. Often they don't have a clear image of their same-sexed parent, and thus seek in others the behavioral reference points they need in order to develop an adequate self image. They are more than followers; they try to *become* like others with whom they relate. They generally are totally unaware that they are doing this.

How to Increase a Child's Sense of Models

Improving a child's sense of Models requires a good deal of patience. Changing models and images that a child has requires that new models for his behavior produce more satisfaction and success than his old ones. In the light of the fact that children with Models problems have difficulty organizing themselves, learning, and setting goals, parents and teachers should be ready to work on this condition, anticipating that they might not see immediate results from their efforts.

- **Help children understand what they believe.** The values and beliefs that children have can act as guides to their behavior. Helping a child to *talk about beliefs* helps him clarify them, and makes them more usable. Children's beliefs change frequently, and parents need to recognize that a commitment may change. Living up to what one believes requires some degree of self discipline, restraint, and conscious decisions about one's actions. This process builds a sense of Models in children.

- **Share what you believe with children.** In their continuing search for making sense of their world, children need reference points provided by the adults they would most like to love and trust—their parents and teachers. Sharing your beliefs with children does not necessarily mean holding them accountable for acting according to what you believe. It only means that they are given some clear messages about your own values and attitudes, so that they can test them with their own experience. When children know where parents stand they can make better choices about their own behavior.

- **Help children set reasonable and achievable goals for themselves.** Human beings, by and large, are goal oriented creatures. Children with Models problems are *not* goal-less, they are confused and unsure about what their goals are. They need considerable help to clarify and work toward simple objectives: "Take your dirty clothes out of the closet, *then* make your bed." It is most helpful for them to have short-term goals, related to things they have to do. Often parents need only help them clarify what they have to do anyhow: "Now, what is it that you're trying to do?" Low Models children need help to set goals for their *behavior* ("How are you going to act when we get to Grandma's house?"), *learning* ("How many math problems are you going to do tonite?"), and tasks or chores ("Which part of your room are you going to work on first; then which part?"). It is sometimes difficult for parents to remember the degree of confusion these children experience in setting reasonable goals. Trying to have such children define global or long-range goals often leads to frustration.

- **Help children to understand the consequences of their behavior.** Children with a low sense of Models have trouble identifying "cause and effect." They are not sure that "A" leads to "B," etc. They appear to be stupid and can easily be labeled as less than bright: "Didn't you know that was going to happen when you opened the window?" They need frequent explanations about how what they do affects others, and need help to foresee the consequences of any intended actions. This is best done by challenging them to think about what they have to do, helping them understand alternatives that they might have, and giving them feedback, in a non-judgmental way, about what they have done. Of course, they can't be watched all the time. But if you try to help them in this way *and* do other things that are explained in this section, you can move the child toward developing a better sense of Models.

- **Let children know what you expect, and make performance standards clear.** Because of the problems described in the last section, low Models children do not often meet reasonable standards of performance in school or at home. While laziness or stupidity may appear to be the reason, more often it is the lack of clarity about standards. Setting appropriate standards clearly is an important task for parents of all children; for low Models children, it is an absolute necessity. It helps when standards are consistent, and reinforced: "No, your room is not done; there should be *no* papers left on the floor. Remember that I told you that the last time?" If they do a good job of something, they should know why: "You did a good job on the lawn. I was especially happy to see that you put the tools away. That's always an important part of a job." It's always a bit "dangerous" to leave important decisions to a low Models child's "good sense." This usually means that we expect a child to know what we want without spelling it out, and children with a low sense of Models *do* need it spelled out.

- **Be a good model for children.** No discussion of a sense of Models can overlook this factor. Since low Models children tend to easily mimic what others do, they also may demonstrate some of their parents' least wholesome behavior and attitudes. Many parents believe that children should "Do as I say; don't do as I do." But children, especially if they have a low sense of Models, tend not to. Being a good model has a more specific meaning than just trying to be a "saint." This is the need to demonstrate to low Models children what you want them to do. *Showing is better than telling.* "Walk" as well as talk them through a task. You may have to show them how to make a bed several times, before they get the hang of it. Complex chores, such as dishwashing, will require you to work with them a number of times before they're ready to try it on their own. If you want them to improve in relating to people, you may have to role-play a little with them. Make it a game, and give them specific lines to say.

  Their competence in human situations is especially important. *How* to relate to others is *learned,* even though the *need* to relate is born into a child. Children with a low sense of Models are often a little, sometimes a lot, "off" in relating. They make others uneasy, because their manner of relating seems strained or awkward. They're trying to do it "right," without being really sure how. This will show up as laughing a bit more than is appropriate, being more or less enthusiastic than a situation calls for, being "too" lovey, etc. They are either too much or too little of something, and other people, including their peers, sense it. Reinforcing, by praise, the times when they do well in relating is an important way to help them make sense out of what they do. The most important help you can give them is to help them review what happens when something goes wrong in their relationships with others.

- **Help children broaden their range of experience.** Children with a low sense of Models tend to need their experience enriched, overall. Since they learn best from being shown, almost any kind of experience that is associated with strong positive behavior will aid them in developing a better sense of Models. Increasing the diversity of their experiences with *people* is important, especially if you also discuss these experiences with them, as a way of helping them make sense of the similarities and differences among people. Out-of-school classes, club activities, sports, etc. are good, especially if conducted by adults who can be patient and tolerant of their "slowness."

Almost any experience is an opportunity for learning. Low Models children profit from watching parents do things, and need exposure to a wide range of things, from every-day tasks, to special things that parents do that may be work-connected. Again, parents need to be forewarned that these children may not "get it" the first few times that parents give explanations about some activity, but allowing them to observe will add to their sense of Models.

Parents teach children primarily by exposing them to experience. In this way any parent can be an effective teacher. Low Models children may be reluctant to enter into new experiences and will need encouragement, which is often best done by offering them something *they* want, an ice cream cone, a special treat, etc., for doing something that *you* want. "Bribing" children to do something that will be good for them is not really a bad idea.

Increasing Order in Your Family

Creating a family climate that enhances a sense of Models depends on three issues:

- **Communications:** Especially regarding rules and limits, standards for performance, and expectations about how people in the family should relate to each other.

- **Planning:** This includes making promises and keeping them, making goals, both short and long-range, clear, and letting people know *how* things are to be done.

- **Keeping order:** Physical surroundings that are orderly are important, promoting good habits through chores, and scheduling family activities so that the important things get done.

These three factors all contribute to helping family members "make sense" out of all the things that happen in the family. If done well, they provide a "structure of experience" that is the basis for a sense of Models. They enable all members of the family to know what is expected of them, to make predictions about the consequences of their actions, to make decisions that they can reasonably expect to carry out, to know what people mean, and to feel secure that parents won't be excessively arbitrary and inconsistent.

Communicating clearly is a skill—one that can be learned, if necessary. It is of the utmost importance that rules and limits be made clear to all members of the family—both those who have to live by them, i.e. everyone, and those who have to enforce them, i.e. parents. Consider what it might be like if traffic laws were left to the whim of every police officer or if they could be changed without informing people. It's doubtful that you would want to venture out in a car. Likewise, when family rules are unclear, changeable, or when parents don't agree on them, an enormous amount of confusion and conflict occurs. Parents need to talk about family rules, and those that apply to individuals, in such a way that everyone understands them. You must check to see that what you said is understood the way you meant it: "Will you please repeat to me what I just said to you?" The greatest confusion can result from lack of clarity about the meaning of two simple words, "yes" and "no." If parents don't mean what they say, what can a child depend on? If children can't be sure about what a parent means, and whether they will follow through on what they've said, their sense of Models is undermined.

Children need to know what's expected of them. They find out by what parents say, how consistent they are, and what response they get when they do or don't live up to expectations. It usually takes a bit more time to communicate clearly, since good communications are always two way—talking and listening. Anyone can tell children what to do; you have to *listen* to them in order to know whether they've heard you or what it is they've missed. When rules and limits are not clear, when they can be changed arbitrarily, or when they are not applied consistently and fairly, then everyone, including parents, becomes anxious and resentful. Living under conditions that are confusing results in feeling confused—the basic symptom of a poor sense of Models.

Planning, as we use the word, is an ongoing process in a family, not something reserved for "big" events. It means that everyone in the family, as much as possible, should know what's going to happen, when, why, and how it's to be done. Toddlers make "plans" that depend on parents' activities: "I want to go to the beach!" Older children are even more autonomous: "Gee, why didn't you tell me we were going shopping? I told Joey that I'd come over to his house." To the extent that members of the family know what's happening, each one can make better decisions about his or her own activities.

Good planning by parents is something that children observe and emulate. Since the ability to plan is an important ingredient of a high sense of Models, providing them with a good example has a profound influence on their self-esteem. Even more to the point—how can adults feel confident about family matters if they can't predict what's going to happen? Unless parents exercise some control over their own *and* children's activities, the resulting confusion diminishes their self-esteem too.

Children need to have lots of "plans" about everyday activities. Unless they have a plan for taking the garbage out, they're likely to do it incorrectly. How to do many ordinary things in a household result from a plan. Can Dad depend on dinner being served at 6:00? How long he stays at the office may depend on being able to predict such things. What's the plan for dealing with soiled clothing—is there a procedure for handling it?

Keeping order within the family involves more than keeping children from fighting with each other. Order is a state of mind that's translated into activities. Orderliness is a personal characteristic that is adopted by "osmosis"—it occurs naturally when people live within orderly surroundings. Being orderly does not mean that a family is never spontaneous or messy; it only means that disorder is not the usual standard. In addition, there are many practical benefits of orderliness. Quite simply, people can find what they need more easily! Parents are less likely to have to clean up after others if standards of neatness are upheld. There is often less tension in the home, because periods of work and play are more clearly distinguished. Furthermore, orderliness has an aesthetic aspect that promotes interest and concern for beauty in one's surroundings.

Children learn orderly habits and develop a high sense of Models by doing required chores at a reasonable standard that is set by parents. Children's participation in keeping things organized through chores and duties is the way that external order becomes a personal characteristic. It is *not* sufficient for parents to keep things neat, clean and well organized for children to develop a good sense of Models. The children must have the experience of performing the necessary tasks. Experience is the basis of a good sense of Models.

Parents who insist that messiness or disorder is more "natural" than good organization, may not themselves pay a price for it, but children will suffer. Adults have a much higher capability for keeping things clear in their own minds than children do: "Leave my messy desk alone; I know where everything is, except when you straighten it up!" What may be "orderly confusion" to parents, may only be confusion to a child.

Keeping order is the result of problem solving, and thus is something that children also learn from parents. Helping a child organize his room is a concrete way of teaching problem solving: "Where would you like to keep your toy soldiers?" As orderly habits become second nature to a child, the sense of Models becomes firm. Even though he may depart from the orderliness at different periods of childhood or adolescence, the basic pattern that exists in the family will eventually assert itself.

Scheduling family activities is another important way in which order is maintained. Having some fixed times is important, meals and bedtimes for example, so that family members can adjust their activities around them, and so that *departures from them are clear.* It's easy for parents to believe that schedules are for their convenience, but children depend on them too, even if they complain about them. Rigid schedules, which are never altered, make no more sense than no schedules. Predictability needs to be high, but not absolute.

* * * * *

NOTE: This handbook is a map that will help you find your route to new territory. And like a map, it must be supplemented by your own observation. Watching what your children do, and listening to what they say are two of the most important links to increasing your understanding of the messages contained in their behavior. We hope that by using the information presented you will become a better "map-reader," and thus be able to help your children, and yourself, with less confusion and stress.

As you have read this handbook, it's very likely that you found yourself reflecting on the degree to which many of the ideas about self-esteem applied to yourself, as well as your children. This only reflects the fact that you and your children share a common humanity, which is the basis of your being able to understand them. Recognizing their common humanity does not mean that you and your children are alike, but that the needs each of you have are not so dissimilar. Acknowledging your own needs, and accepting them, can help you have patience and compassion for their efforts to realize high self-esteem.

—The Authors

Notes

[1]See: *How to Teach Children Responsibility* (Bean and Clemes) Enrich, 1980.

[2]See: *Setting Limits and Rules for Children* (Clemes and Bean) Enrich, 1980.

NOTES

NOTES

NOTES

NOTES

NOTES

NOTES

TEACHER/PARENT RESOURCE BOOKS

• DISCIPLINE • RESPONSIBILITY • SELF-ESTEEM

These Resource Books offer practical techniques for dealing with children who have learning and/or behavioral problems. The books are written in an easy to understand, straight-forward style. They offer sound advice from family counselors in the areas that are most important to improving children's school performance.

Reynold Bean, Ed.M.   Harris Clemes, Ph.D.

HOW TO RAISE CHILDREN'S SELF-ESTEEM
This handbook shows how to help children improve: Self-confidence–Values and attitudes–Interaction with others.

HOW TO RAISE TEENAGERS' SELF-ESTEEM
Case examples illustrate: New approaches to teenager problems–Analyses of self-esteem problems–Guides to raising self-esteem.

HOW TO DISCIPLINE CHILDREN WITHOUT FEELING GUILTY
Adults can learn to direct children effectively by: Rewarding good behavior–Fitting chores to the child–Being consistent with discipline.

HOW TO TEACH CHILDREN RESPONSIBILITY
This handbook defines responsibility and provides practical activities for teaching responsibility: Helps children solve problems in school and at home.